Come Here, Puppy

by Michèle Dufresne

Literacy Footprints, Inc.

"Come here," said Bella.

"No!" said the little puppy.

"Come here," said Rosie.
"Come here!"

"No! No! No!" said the little puppy.

"Come here," said Rosie.

"Come here," said Bella.

"No!" said the little puppy.

"No! No! No!"

"Come here," said Rosie.

"Come here," said Bella.

"No!" said the little puppy.

"Yes!" said Bella and Rosie.